WILLIMENA RULES!

RULE BOOK #1
How to Lose Your Class Pet

By Valerie Wilson Wesley
Illustrated by Maryn Roos

JUMP AT THE SUN
HYPERION BOOKS FOR CHILDREN • NEW YORK

For the kids at the Whitney E. Houston Academy

Text copyright © 2003 by Valerie Wilson Wesley
Illustrations copyright © 2003 by Maryn Roos

For information please address Hyperion Books for Children,
114 Fifth Avenue, New York,
New York 10011-5690.

Printed in the United States

First Edition

3 5 7 9 10 8 6 4 2

Library of Congress Cataloging-in-Publication Data on file

ISBN 0-7868-1322-9

Visit www.hyperionchildrensbooks.com

My Rules Step-by-Step

Step #1: Begin the First Day of School with a Burp!

It was the first day of school, and my sister Tina and I were eating breakfast.

"You might be in the third grade now, but you're still not as grown as me," Tina said. She'll be in the fifth grade this year, and she never lets me forget it. She shoveled *five* forkfuls of pancakes into her mouth and started to chew with her mouth open. Tina knows I hate that.

My mom had just left for work. My dad

1

was still upstairs. Our baby-sitter, Mrs. Cotton, hadn't arrived yet. Tina and I were in the kitchen alone. It was the perfect time for a fight.

"You don't *eat* like somebody grown," I said. Tina opened her mouth so wide I could see everything in it. Then she dabbed her mouth with a napkin like they do on TV.

Then I did something that Tina hates worse than broccoli. I took a gulp of orange juice.

Then I burped like my cousin Teddy taught me to do last summer.

"Yuck! Yuck! You are really disgusting, Willie!" Tina screamed.

"So are you, miss thinks-she-is-grown Tina Thomas," I said.

"You are such a *baby*, Willie."

I hate it when Tina calls me a baby. I hate it worse than she hates my burping.

"Don't call me a baby!" I gave her my meanest look.

"Fifth graders are more grown than *baby* third graders," Tina said.

I took a tiny, neat nibble of my pancakes and said, "Fifth graders aren't as grown as seventh graders."

"But fifth grade is better than third grade," Tina said. "Second grade is the only thing worse than third grade."

I knew she was right. And worse than second grade was first grade.

The only grade even worse than that was kindergarten, where the *real* babies were.

"Shut up, Tina," I said.

"You started it," Tina said.

"No I didn't!"

"Yes you did!"

"Baby, baby, baby, baby!" Tina said.

"Girls! Stop that arguing right now!" my dad said as he came downstairs. "Here it is the first day of school, and you two are fighting again! You really are the Sisters Umoja." Tina and I looked at each other and then we started to laugh. *Umoja* means "unity" in Swahili. My dad calls us that whenever we fight, which is all the time.

"You and Willie are *both* my big girls. I want you *both* to act that way. I want you to make your first day of school a great one. Okay?"

At that moment, our doorbell rang. Tina shoved another forkful of pancakes into her mouth. I took a sip of orange juice. We knew it was Mrs. Cotton.

Sometimes Mrs. Cotton is nice, but usually she is grumpy.

"Good morning, little Thomases!" Mrs. Cotton said.

"Good morning, Mrs. Cotton," I said.

"I know you two are looking forward to the first day of school," Mrs. Cotton said.

Tina and I didn't say anything.

What kind of kid looks forward to the first day of school?

"Would you like some breakfast, Mrs. Cotton?" my dad asked.

"No, but I hate to waste food," Mrs. Cotton said, looking in my direction. Then she picked up my glass of juice, which was almost full. "I'll just finish up this juice for Willimena. You don't mind, do you, honey?

And how *are* the little Thomases this bright morning?"

"Just fine, Mrs. Cotton," Tina said.

I didn't say anything. I was mad at Mrs. Cotton for drinking my orange juice. Nobody had ever done that to me before, not even Tina.

Mrs. Cotton patted Tina on the head. "You are such a nice, grown-up, lovely little lady, Tina. Such a nice, polite little lady," she said.

"Thank you, Mrs. Cotton," Tina said.

"Aren't you proud of your *big, grown* daughter, Mr. Thomas? She's certainly not a baby anymore," Mrs. Cotton said to my dad. Then she looked at me. "I hope you will grow up into a nice, polite young lady like your big sister," she said.

I shouldn't have done what I did next.

But I couldn't stop myself. I think it was because Mrs. Cotton drank my orange juice and said the "b-word" all in the same three minutes.

I burped.

Teddy would have been proud of me. It was the loudest burp I'd ever done.

Mrs. Cotton put her hand over her heart. She gasped. She glared at me. "Rude! Rude! Rude! Willimena Thomas!" she said.

My dad threw me a warning look.

"Please excuse me," I said. I didn't really mean it. I was just sorry that I had angered my father.

"That's better," Mrs. Cotton said approvingly.

"I'm proud of both my daughters, Mrs. Cotton," my dad said. He probably guessed that my feelings were hurt about the orange juice and the "b-word." He glanced at his watch. "Come on, Sisters Umoja, I'll walk you two to the bus."

"Hey, Tina. Hey, Willie," Gregory Greene said when we got to the bus stop. Gregory's in seventh grade this year. He was standing beside Crawford Mills. I tried to move behind Tina so Crawford Mills wouldn't see me, but it was too late.

Crawford Mills had been in my second-grade class last year. Every time he got a chance, he made fun of me. If I made a mistake, he laughed. He even laughed when I fell on the ice in front of my house.

"Hey, it's Silly Willie Thomas," he said.

I felt like melting into the sidewalk.

"Crawford Mills, you'd better leave my sister alone!" Tina said. Her voice was loud.

She put her hand on her hips. She thrust out her chin and wriggled her shoulders. She sounded tough, like a big-time fifth grader.

But Crawford Mills wasn't going to be put down that easily, even by a fifth grader. "You think you're in Mrs. Jones's class, don't you?" he said to me.

"Yeah," I said. I was so glad that Mrs. Jones was going to be my teacher. I knew Crawford was going to be in Mrs. Sweetly's class. I was happy he wouldn't be in my class again.

"You got it wrong," Crawford said.

"But that's what my teacher told me at the end of last year!" I said.

"That shows how much you know, Silly Willie Thomas," said Crawford. "Mrs. Jones is having a baby, so she won't be back this year. All the kids in her class whose last names start with T are going to be in Mrs. Sweetly's class. So you're in Mrs. Sweetly's class just like me." Crawford laughed so hard he doubled over. Then he stood back up and laughed again.

I gasped and looked at Tina. She sighed and dropped her eyes to the ground. My first day in the third grade had turned into a disaster.

Step #2:
Be Afraid, Very Afraid, of Your Third-Grade Teacher

Mrs. Sweetly was the meanest teacher in the Harriet Tubman School. In all my years at Tubman, I had never seen Mrs. Sweetly laugh. Tina told me that she had seen her smile once, but it hadn't been for long. And now I was going to be in the lady's class.

The worst thing was, I had teased Crawford Mills about his bad luck at the end of last year.

"Serves you right! Serves you right!" I

sang to Crawford when I found out he had Mrs. Sweetly. And now I'd be sitting right beside him. In mean Mrs. Sweetly's class. With the rest of the losers.

When I got to school, I stood in the hall in front of the picture of Harriet Tubman for a few minutes. Harriet Tubman is my personal hero.

She lived during the time when African Americans were enslaved. She rescued them from the South and brought them North on the Underground Railroad. I used to think that the Underground Railroad was like a subway. I thought you could put a token in the slot in Charleston and get off in Boston. But my dad set me straight.

The Underground Railroad was made up of people who fought against slavery and helped enslaved people escape. Harriet

Tubman was called the "conductor" of the Underground Railroad because she led so many people to freedom. She was a very brave person. Just looking at her picture makes me feel brave. When I thought about all the scary things that Harriet Tubman had to face, I felt dumb being afraid to walk into Mrs. Sweetly's class.

Just as the first bell rang Tina took my hand and held it. We were supposed to be sitting in our seats by second bell, or you could end up in Mrs. Morris's office. She's the vice principal, and you sure don't want to end up spending the morning with her. She is even worse than Mrs. Sweetly. Imagine that!

"Do you want me to walk you there?" she asked.

"Of course not!" I said. That would be

the worst thing that could happen, to have
to be walked to class by your big sister. I'd
never live it down.

"See you on the bus tonight," I said, trying to sound brave.

"See you," Tina said, and we both ran, trying to beat the bell.

I made it into Mrs. Sweetly's classroom just as the second bell rang. She was standing behind her desk. She had a scowl on her face. She looked at me. Then she looked at the clock. Then she looked at me again. Nobody moved. Nobody spoke.

"And you are?" Mrs. Sweetly asked. Her lips barely moved.

I couldn't find my voice.

"Willimena Thomas!" Crawford Mills yelled out. Mrs. Sweetly turned to look at him. Her eyes were as cold as a snake's.

She stared at him, and then she said, "Children do not speak out of turn in my classroom. Never!"

"I—I—I am—Willie Thomas," I finally stuttered. My knees were shaking.

"Please find your place among the T's," Mrs. Sweetly said.

"Welcome to my class, people. You are in the third grade now, and I expect you to act accordingly," she said.

Then she told us the rules of her class-room:

1. No talking unless asked.
2. Only one person to go to the rest room at a time.
3. No snacking in class.

They were the same rules we got every year. No surprises there.

"Now it's time for us to get to work," Mrs. Sweetly said. We knew she meant business. She held up some small blue notebooks.

"You will use these notebooks as your journals," she said as she passed them out. "Each night, I want you to write down your thoughts. Writing in your journals will be an ongoing homework assignment. Each morning I will collect your journals, and I will give them back to you at the end of the day.

"I would like you to write the truth. I promise that nobody will read your journals but me. Sometimes I will write my thoughts about what you've said. Sometimes I won't. But please feel free to tell me what you really feel."

"No way! No way! I ain't telling that woman my business!" whispered Linda Turner, who sat in the chair next to me.

"Me, neither," said Bill Taylor. "She doesn't want to know what I think about her."

I didn't say anything because I love to write. Keeping a journal sounded like it might be fun.

The rest of the day went on like every other. But near the end of it, something exciting finally happened.

Squeak, squeak, squeak! A funny screeching sound came from the back of the room. Everybody looked up from their books. Nobody knew what it was. Then we heard the sound again.

Squeak! Squeak! Squeak! A kid started to laugh. Pretty soon the whole class was laughing. Then the impossible happened. Mrs. Sweetly started to smile. It was a tiny smile at first. Then it grew into a genuine grin. Then she laughed out loud.

"There is one thing about our class I forgot to mention," she said. "That one thing is Lester. You just heard him. Lester is a Peruvian guinea pig. He is our class pet."

"Wow, a class pet," Linda Turner whispered. "Maybe Mrs. Sweetly's class won't be so bad after all."

Before we went home, Mrs. Sweetly reminded us to write in our journals. I grabbed my sweater and backpack and headed for the door as fast as I could go. I glanced at Lester's cage, but all I could see was his furry little body. I didn't know if I was looking at his front or his back.

Step #3: Get Mad at Everyone

After school, Tina and I went to the Greenes' backyard. There are five kids in the Greene family. They all have names that start with G, beginning with the oldest, Gregory Greene, and continuing through George (my least-favorite Greene!) and Grace and Gerry to baby Ginger.

Pauline, who lives across the street, came over too.

"How do you like your new teacher?" Pauline asked Tina.

"She's the nicest teacher in the whole

world!" Tina said. "I'm so glad I have her instead of a mean teacher." I wondered if Tina was trying to rub it in about Mrs. Sweetly.

"You know what I love best about my teacher?" Tina continued. "I love the way she calls everybody 'darling' even though we're in the fifth grade. Like she'll say, 'Come on, darling,' you can read that,' or 'Don't be afraid to try it, darling.' Isn't that nice?"

"My teacher is nice, too," Pauline said. "She smells like flowers, and she brought cupcakes with sprinkles for the whole class today!"

"Wow! Aren't we lucky to have nice teachers?" Tina said.

"Shut up, Tina!" I said.

She and Pauline looked at me in surprise.

"Shut up, yourself," Tina said. "It's not our fault you have mean Mrs. Sweetly."

"Shut up! I mean it!" I said.

Tina turned up her nose. She and Pauline moved to the other side of the yard. After they left, I was sorry I'd told Tina to

shut up. But sometimes she gets on my nerves.

"Hey, everybody!" Amber and Lydia yelled as they ran into the yard, and I felt better. Amber is my best friend. She goes to a different school than we do, so she doesn't know Mrs. Sweetly. Lena and Lana, the twins who live a couple of houses down from me, came into the backyard, too.

After a while, Amber sat down beside me. "Tina told Lydia about Mrs. Sweetly, and Lydia told me. Is she *really* mean?" she asked.

"Well, she wasn't really mean, but she wasn't really nice either," I said.

"But teachers are *always* nice the first day," Amber said.

"She was just . . . okay," I said. "But she really likes the class guinea pig."

"You have a class pet? Wow! You're so lucky. That's *so-o-o* nice," said Amber.

Maybe there was something good about Mrs. Sweetly's class after all.

"He's really adorable," I said.

"What's his name?"

"Lester."

"That's such an *adorable* name! I have a cousin named Lester."

"Have you held him yet?" Lena and Lana chimed in. They both love animals, but their aunt won't let them have one because she is allergic to fur.

"Can you—?"

"Bring him home?" Lena finished her sister's sentence.

"Maybe," I said. I hadn't thought about that.

Crawford Mills pushed in front of Lena.

He must have been listening to us talking for a while. I didn't see him come into the Greenes' backyard.

"Are you talking about that ugly, smelly old guinea pig?" he asked.

"How do you know Lester smells?" I asked.

"Because *everybody* knows he smells. He smells and he's mean, just like Mrs. Sweetly."

"You're dumb for saying Lester smells when you don't know!" I said. "And what makes you think he's mean?"

"Because he bit a kid in kindergarten last year!" Crawford said.

Lena and Lana gasped.

"They were going to get rid of him, but Mrs. Sweetly said she'd keep him because third graders would know how to handle him. That's how come he's in our room. Trust silly Willie Thomas to like an evil old guinea pig!" said Crawford Mills.

"No, I don't," I said.

"Just like you like mean Mrs. Sweetly," he said.

"I don't know if Mrs. Sweetly is mean or not," I said.

Some more kids had gathered around. Crawford threw out his chin and squinted his eyes. "There are only two ways to act with a mean teacher," he said. "You can either be a goody-goody teacher's pet and do whatever she says, or you can stand up and let her know who's the boss."

"Mrs. Sweetly *is* the boss. She's the teacher," said Gregory Greene. "And you'd better watch yourself, or you'll get into trouble."

"Don't you children have homework?" Mrs. Greene called out from the back porch.

"Ma, it's the first day of school!" said Grace Greene.

"Well, it's time for everybody to go home, anyway," Mrs. Greene said. "My children have chores to do."

So we all went home. But I began to think that some of what Crawford said made sense. Did a kid have to be a goody-goody teacher's pet to get along with Mrs. Sweetly, or stand up and let her know who's the boss? I knew where Crawford Mills stood. But what about me?

Step #4: Never Tell Anyone Your Secret Plan

That night when I started my homework, I was glad that writing in my new journal was the only thing I had to do. I thought about what Mrs. Sweetly had said about telling the truth. And I thought about what Crawford had said about Mrs. Sweetly and Lester. I wrote in my very best handwriting:

> I love Lester! He is a very nice guinea pig. He's so cute! I'm very, very, very happy that he is in our third-grade class.

I didn't know yet if that was the truth,

but I decided to give Lester the benefit of the doubt.

Because it was the first day of school, my dad made chocolate sundaes for dessert. I was stuffed when I went to bed. Maybe that was why I couldn't fall asleep. But I was also worried about what would happen in Mrs. Sweetly's class.

I thought about what Crawford had said. I knew exactly what he meant when he'd talked about being the boss. Crawford was tough. He wasn't afraid of a fight.

I'm not like Crawford Mills. I hate to fight—except with Tina. I'd never hit anybody—except Tina. When somebody shoves me, I'm afraid to shove back—except Tina. I never shove first.

There was no way I could ever stand up to Mrs. Sweetly like Crawford.

"You still awake?" Tina asked after a while.

"Yeah," I said as softly as I could.

"Are you worried about being in Mrs. Sweetly's class?" Tina asked.

"No!"

"Yes, you are," said Tina.

"I just don't want her to get mad at me," I said.

"How are you going to stop her?" Tina asked.

I thought about that for a long while, then said, "I'm going to do everything I can to make her like me. I'll smile all the time. I'll never say anything to make her frown. I'll be the nicest kid she's ever had in her class."

"What do you mean?" Tina asked.

"I'm going to be super nice, super good,

32

super sweet," I said.

"That's disgusting!" she said.

"What's disgusting about it?"

"Just being nice to get on a teacher's good side is like lying," Tina said.

"But I don't want her to yell at me," I said.

"Being super nice is pretending to be something you're not," Tina said.

"At least I won't get into trouble," I said.

"There is nothing worse in the world than a kid who tries to be a teacher's pet by pretending to be super nice when everybody knows the way she is in real life," Tina said. "Well, if you do it, don't tell anybody you're my sister. I don't want to be embarrassed." I heard her snatch the blanket over her head, which is what Tina does when she's tired of talking.

"Don't worry, I won't!" I snapped. But I don't think she heard me.

Just to make sure I had the last word, I turned the page in my journal and wrote:

Sometimes my sister just doesn't understand me.

Step #5: Volunteer for Everything

The next morning in Mrs. Sweetly's class, I was eager to play my new role. When she frowned at the class, I frowned. She scowled at Crawford Mills, and I scowled at him too. When she smiled, I smiled. When she asked a question, I answered first. When Mrs. Sweetly asked for a volunteer, I raised my hand before anybody else.

"My, Willie, you are a very hard worker," Mrs. Sweetly said.

"Thank you, Mrs. Sweetly," I said. My lips

were starting to hurt from smiling so much.

When Mrs. Sweetly wasn't looking, Crawford stuck his tongue out at me. I ignored him.

"Today, class, I will assign class chores," Mrs. Sweetly said before lunch. "First of all, I need somebody to erase the boards at the end of the day."

"I'll do it!" I called out.

"Thank you, Willie," she said.

"I need a volunteer to pass out our workbooks for reading and math."

"I'll do it!" I yelled out. Several kids in the class gave me mean looks. I tried not to see them.

"But, Willie, you've already volunteered for something," Mrs. Sweetly said.

"I just like to be helpful, Mrs. Sweetly," I said very *sweetly*.

Crawford made a weird sound in the back of his throat. Nobody heard it but me.

"Thank you, Willie, but there are many children in our class. This time I'll choose somebody else," she said.

On our way to lunch, Crawford caught up with me even though I tried to walk fast. I knew he would have something mean to say. I was right.

"'I like to be helpful, Mrs. Sweetly!'" he said in a sickening, sweet voice.

"Shut up, Crawford!"

"'I like to be helpful, Mrs. Sweetly!'" Crawford said again. "Willimena Thomas likes to be helpful!" he said loud enough for anybody who was walking behind us to hear. A kid giggled, and I remembered what Tina had said about just trying to get on Mrs. Sweetly's good side.

At the end of the day, Mrs. Sweetly asked for one more volunteer. "I need a very special volunteer now," she said. "I need somebody to take care of Lester, our pet guinea pig."

"Yuck," somebody said from the back row.

"Forget that!" Crawford said.

"His caretaker will need to give him food and water each morning, and change the bedding in his cage," Mrs. Sweetly said. "Does anybody in the class know anything about guinea pigs?"

Nobody said anything, so Mrs. Sweetly continued. "First of all, guinea pigs are not really pigs. They are rodents."

"So Lester is just a big, fat rat!" Crawford whispered.

Mrs. Sweetly gave him a warning look.

"Guinea pigs come in many breeds. Lester is a Peruvian guinea pig. You may have noticed that he has very long silky hair," she continued, and then opened Lester's cage and gently picked him up. It was the first time that anybody had gotten a good look at him.

He was about eight inches long. He had tiny ears, no tail, and he was covered with brown silky hair that fell over his face and back. It was hard to tell which end was which.

"Because Lester has long hair, the person who cares for him weekly will need to brush him, and he must be handled very gently," Mrs. Sweetly added.

"His water bottle must be filled daily, and he must be given rabbit-food pellets.

We also have to feed him fresh vegetables. Who would like to take care of Lester?" she asked.

Besides me, five kids raised their hands. But then Mrs. Sweetly looked at me

Who would like to take care of Lester?

and smiled. I knew it was because I said I liked to be helpful. She said I could take care of him the first week. It was the best news I'd had all day! My secret plan was working.

That night, after I'd done my homework, I wrote in my journal.

> I love Lester! Mrs. Sweetly's class is going to be great! This is going to be the best class I've ever had!

Boy, was I in for a surprise.

Step #6: Agree to Bring Your Class Pet Home

I've never been responsible for a pet before. Everybody in our family takes care of our cat Doofus Doolittle. But Lester was *my* responsibility.

I looked forward to feeding him every morning. I loved putting water in his bottle. I didn't mind cleaning his cage. But there was one thing that bothered me. Most pets are nice. Lester wasn't.

For one thing, he didn't seem to notice the extra lettuce I brought from home.

When I gave him a piece of carrot in the morning, he'd snatch it out of my hand with his sharp little teeth and run as fast as he could under his shoe-box house.

Other pets let a kid know that they like her. Doofus Doolittle sits on my lap and licks my hand. Casey, George Greene's dog, runs in circles when George comes home from school. The least Lester could do was look me in the eye. Was that too much to ask?

Mrs. Sweetly gave me a book about guinea pigs so I'd learn more about them. But Lester wasn't like the guinea pigs in the book. I asked my dad to help me find more information, so we went online on our computer.

One of the things we found out was that guinea pigs are also called "cavies." The scientific name is *Cavia porcellus*. Several sites said that guinea pigs first came from the Andes Mountains in South America, and that they were probably raised for food. I screamed out loud when we read that. Even though Lester was unfriendly, I didn't want to think that somebody ate his ancestors for lunch.

I also found out that guinea pigs like to live in high grass, which is their natural habitat. They love peace and quiet and when they're startled by loud noises or sudden movements, they stand perfectly still. Sometimes they don't move for twenty minutes!

I quickly discovered that I needed to clean Lester's cage almost every day or the kids in my class would hold their noses and complain. Lester also drank a lot of water and ate a lot. Every time I looked at him, he was stuffing his mouth. Maybe that was why they call them guinea *pigs*.

Thursday morning, Mrs. Sweetly said that I had done a good job of taking care of Lester. She wanted to know if I'd like to take Lester home for the weekend. She wrote a note home to my mom that night. The next day, my mom wrote back that I could bring him home. So after school on Friday, Mrs. Sweetly carried Lester's cage to the bus with me.

Mrs. Cotton met the bus, and carried Lester's cage home. I could tell she didn't want to carry Lester. She kept wrinkling up her nose. She put Lester on our back porch. I moved his cage into our backyard so he could see the grass through his cage.

And so began the worst weekend of my life.

Step #7: Set Up the Escape

The moment I put Lester's cage in our yard, the kids from my block gathered around and started talking at the same time.

"Please, let me touch him!"

"Oh, he's *so-o-o* cute!"

"Where's his face?"

"Please, can I hold him? Please, Willie! Please!"

Everybody wanted to see Lester. Everybody wanted to pet him. Everybody was pushing, pleading, and talking loud.

I felt so sorry for Lester. He ran into his little shoe-box home inside of his cage to get away from the crowd.

Everybody was yelling:

"Hey, where did he go?" "We want to see him!" "Take out that shoe box!"

That was when I did what I never should have done. I listened to the crowd. I opened the cage and lifted out the shoe box. Lester stood perfectly still.

"Looks like he's about to croak!" said Crawford Mills, who had come over from the Greenes' backyard.

"He's fine. That's what guinea pigs do when they get scared. They don't move. They freeze," I said. I was glad I knew the facts.

"That's dumb. Why doesn't he just run away?" said Crawford, who never accepts

anything as true unless he says it.

"Where's he going to go?" asked Gregory Greene. "He's trapped in that box." I was glad that Gregory put bigmouthed Crawford Mills in his place.

"So what does he eat?" Gregory asked.

"Pellets mostly," I said. "But he likes lettuce, too."

"Cool," Gregory said. "Can you pick him up?"

"Who would want to pick up a fat rat?" asked Crawford.

"I do!" said Betty, who lives down the street. "Please, Willie, let me hold him!"

"Can we have just—" Lana began.

"One little pat?" said Lena finishing Lana's sentence.

Suddenly everybody was begging. Everyone was pushing. Even Tina.

"One at a time! If everybody is quiet and waits patiently, everybody will have a turn," I said, just like a teacher.

Betty and her little brother Booker were the youngest kids, so I let them go first.

I picked Lester up very carefully. His body was very stiff. I could hardly feel him breathing.

"You can just touch him a little bit,"

I told Betty. She touched him very gently with the tip of her finger.

The twins, Lena and Lana, were in line after Booker, and then Pauline. After Pauline came Amber and Lydia. The Greenes came next. Even Crawford Mills got a turn. Everybody patted the top of Lester's head with their fingertips. He followed everybody around with his eyes, but he didn't move. Finally, I put him back in his cage. He jumped out of the box. The minute his tiny feet hit the shavings, he was happy.

As soon as Lester was back in his cage, everybody went home, and I sighed a sigh of relief. I brought his cage inside and put him on the kitchen floor. Unfortunately, my parents weren't home yet.

"Willimena Thomas, animals belong outside. Do not bring him into this house," Mrs. Cotton said.

"Your mother said nothing to me about allowing little animals inside. Besides, his cage smells like a dirty barn! Please take him outside, little Miss Thomas."

Once Mrs. Cotton had made up her mind about something, it was impossible to make her change it. Then Tina came to the rescue.

"If we clean Lester's cage so it doesn't smell, can Willie take him to our room, Mrs. Cotton?" she asked. Tina put on her cutest smile.

"Well—" Mrs. Cotton paused.

"Please, Mrs. Cotton. Please! Please!" Tina said.

"We'll do such a good job of cleaning his

cage. I promise. Please!" I said, adding my two cents' worth.

Mrs. Cotton kept us on ice for a minute. "All right. But take him straight up to your room, after his cage is cleaned," she finally said.

"Thank you so much, Mrs. Cotton. Thank you!" Tina and I both cheered.

"You're the best baby-sitter ever!" Tina said. I threw Tina a warning look. She was spreading it on a little too thick.

After dinner, we gathered up some old newspapers and tore them into tiny pieces. We didn't have any clean cedar shavings for Lester's cage so torn newpaper would have to do.

Then Tina and I carried Lester's cage into the middle of the backyard.

Lester stood perfectly still in the middle

of the cage. He didn't move a muscle.

"Maybe something *is* wrong with him," Tina said softly. I could tell she was worried.

Fear crept over me. Maybe Lester *was* sick. I picked him up very gently. He moved his head and looked at me.

He's okay, I thought. So I gave him a hug and put him back in his cage. Then I took out his water bottle and bowl. I washed both of them, rinsed them clean, and laid them on the grass to dry. Lester still hadn't moved.

"He looks so sad," Tina said with sigh.

"Yeah, he does," I agreed.

"All the kids probably scared him," Tina said.

"Yeah." I was sorry now I had let everybody pet him.

Tina and I both sat on the grass looking at Lester. I'd never seen any animal stand still for so long.

"I wish we could think of something to make him feel better," Tina said. "Maybe he'll feel better when his cage is clean."

"Sure he will," I said. I reached into the cage, picked Lester up, and gave him to Tina. I dumped out all the old shavings and put in the torn newspaper. I put his water bottle and bowl back in the cage. Then I put Lester back in.

He stood where we put him. He didn't move. That's when I remembered what I'd read about a guinea pig's natural habitat.

There's nothing in his cage that smells like grass. He might feel better if he could just play in our grass, I thought.

So, very gently, I lifted him out of his cage.

"Here you are, little dearie," I said, placing him carefully on a patch of grass next to the cage. Dearie is what my grandma calls me when she does something nice for me.

"That's *so-o-o* nice of you," said Tina. I looked up at her and we smiled. Then we started to giggle. And that was when it happened.

In the split second between our smiles and giggles, Lester was gone!

Step #8: Get Everyone's Sympathy

Lester had disappeared into thin air. Tina and I searched everywhere for him. We looked under the porch and between the hedges. We looked in Lydia and Amber's yard. We searched for Lester until it was too dark to see. When my parents came home, my dad got his flashlight and helped us look some more. But Lester was gone.

"I blame Mrs. Cotton," Tina said before we went to sleep that night.

I didn't say anything, because I couldn't blame anybody but myself.

"What am I going to do?" I wailed.

Tina thought a moment and said, "We'll organize a search party tomorrow. We'll look everywhere a guinea pig could hide. We'll find him, Willie, don't worry." Tina sounded so sure about it, I almost believed her.

The next day was Saturday.

"What? No waffles?" my dad asked when Tina and I came down the stairs for breakfast. My dad usually cooks waffles on Saturday. The waffle iron was all ready to go. But I grabbed a banana. Tina bit into an apple.

"We don't have time for breakfast. We have to look for Lester," I told him.

"You shouldn't look on an empty stomach," he said.

"I'm really not hungry, Dad," I said.

61

And that was the truth. I wasn't.

Our first stop was Lydia and Amber's house.

When I told her what had happened, Amber put her hands over mouth as if she were smothering a scream. "Oh, no! Did you forget to lock the cage?"

"No, I put him on the grass so he could have some fun." When I said it, I realized how dumb it sounded. I should have known what would happen.

"It wasn't your fault," Amber said. "Don't blame yourself."

I felt a little better when she said that.

But I could count on Crawford Mills to throw me back into the dumps.

"Wow, Willie. You really blew it this time," he said. He had come into Amber's yard just as I finished telling her what had happened. He had spent the night at the Greenes' house. "You lost the class pet! The class pet! I wouldn't want to be you for cash money!"

Crawford's words made me feel terrible. Suddenly everything that had happened—

You lost the class pet!

and that was about to happen—came crashing down on me.

"Shut up, Crawford Mills. C-l-o-s-e y-o-u-r b-i-g m-o-u-t-h! And that spells 'close your big mouth,'" Tina said. She stared Crawford down, daring him to say anything else.

Amber's older sister joined in. "Willie was just trying to be nice to Lester. Are you going to help us look for him or not?"

Crawford shrugged as if he didn't care. But then he did something that surprised me. He went inside to get his flashlight out of his overnight bag.

"This will help us look in dark places," he said.

Soon everybody on the block had joined the search party. We searched our backyard again. Then we went from house to house.

Crawford got on his knees and shined his flashlight into corners like he said he would. Lena and Lana spread out lettuce and cabbage. Lydia and Amber made up a song that they thought he might like. I made a silent promise to Lester that I would never let anybody pet him again. Nothing worked.

Lunchtime rolled around, and Lester was still missing. My dad made us the waffles he'd promised us for breakfast. I let Tina eat mine when he left the kitchen. I had no appetite.

Tina and I looked outside until it was dark. Then my dad came out and helped us look some more. He helped us look in all of the places we had looked before. Lester's name rang throughout the neighborhood.

Finally it was time to give up the search.

We went out for pizza that night. But I didn't feel like eating pepperoni, cheese, or tomato sauce.

My dad took us to get ice cream at Appleton's after we left the pizzeria. Appleton's makes the best ice cream I've ever eaten. Tina got her favorite, which is cookies 'n' cream with rainbow sprinkles. I took one lick of mine, mint-chocolate-chip with double-chocolate sprinkles, and didn't want any more. My mom said she would wrap it up and put it in the freezer when we got home. I could eat it later when I was feeling better.

As soon as we got home, I ran to the spot where Lester's cage stood. But no Lester. The cage was still empty.

When I came inside, my mom and dad were sitting at the kitchen table. I knew they were talking about what had happened.

"I don't think you're going to find Lester," my mom said. "I think it's time to call Mrs. Sweetly and tell her what happened."

"No! I want to look some more. Maybe he'll still come home. It's only Saturday night. Can we wait some more, please!"

My mom glanced at my dad and sighed. "We'll give Lester one more night, Willie. But then we'll have to call Mrs. Sweetly."

On Sunday morning, Tina and I looked some more. We looked everywhere we had looked before. But it was no use.

Dinnertime came and went, but still no Lester.

So, my mom called Mrs. Sweetly after dinner. I didn't want to hear what she said.

So I turned on the TV, but I didn't watch it. I just stared straight ahead. Soon my mom came in and sat down next to me on the couch.

"I just spoke to Mrs. Sweetly," she said.

"Was she mad?" I was almost too scared to ask. My mom smiled.

"No, of course not," she said.

"Am I going to be suspended?" I was still scared.

"No, Willie." Mom gave me a hug. "Mrs. Sweetly completely understood. She said that when you send a pet home with a child, this is always a possibility."

"But if I hadn't let everybody pet him, if I hadn't put him on the ground, if I hadn't—"

"Willie, this could happen to any child," my mom interrupted me. "Mrs. Sweetly was more concerned about you. She wanted to know how you were taking this. Are you okay?"

"I'm okay," I said. But I wasn't telling the truth. I wasn't okay at all. After I finished my homework, I wrote in my journal:

> Lester ran away. I feel very, very sad because it is my fault. If I hadn't let all the kids on the block pet him he might not have run away. I should have taken better care of him. I should have stood up for Lester's rights and not tried to make everybody like me by letting them pet him. I LET LESTER DOWN!

When I closed my journal, I felt better because I'd written down my thoughts. But not too much better.

"Willie, you shouldn't feel all that bad.

Lester really wasn't all that nice, anyway," Tina said when we were in bed that night.

"You know what else?" Tina continued with a yawn. "Lester is probably happy now. He gets to eat grass whenever he wants it. He can run outside and play. Maybe you did Lester a favor. Go to sleep! You'll feel better tomorrow."

I didn't want to think about tomorrow. "Tina, what am I going to tell all the kids at school?" I asked, but Tina didn't answer.

Maybe she was already asleep. Or maybe she just didn't know what to say.

Step #9: Get Over It and Eat Ice Cream

My dad drove us to school on Monday so he could drop off Lester's cage in the school office. Mrs. Sweetly told him to bring it there instead of the classroom. After he left, Mrs. Morris, the vice principal, came out of her office to see how I was feeling. I guess she knew about Lester's getaway. After the last bell rang, she gave me a pass to go to Mrs. Sweetly's class. I took my own sweet time getting there.

I read each and every essay posted on the bulletin board in the hall. I picked up every slip of paper that I found until I reached the third floor. Then, I walked back downstairs to the first floor to get a drink of water from my favorite fountain, the one near the picture of Harriet Tubman.

All in all, it took me about fifteen minutes to get to class. When I walked in, Mrs. Sweetly didn't say anything. She just gave me a sad smile. I put my journal on top of the others on her desk and sank down in my seat.

Lucky for me, it was "quiet time." Everybody was reading their library books while Mrs. Sweetly read our journals. After we finished reading, Mrs. Sweetly passed out our math workbooks and we worked on math problems. Nobody mentioned Lester.

Maybe they wouldn't realize he was gone, I thought. Maybe nobody would say anything.

No such luck.

As we were getting ready to go to lunch, somebody asked the question I'd been dreading

"Hey, where's Lester?" It was Charlie Prentice. I had never heard him say a single word before. Just my luck, he chose today to open his mouth.

"Where Lester's cage?" somebody else asked.

"Where did he go?" another kid yelled.

"He went home with Willie!" somebody volunteered.

"Hey, Willie, when are you going to bring him back?" a fourth kid asked.

I didn't look at anybody. I just tried very hard to sink through my chair into the floor.

"Everybody be quiet, and I will explain what has happened," said Mrs. Sweetly.

"Last weekend, when Willie was cleaning Lester's cage, Lester got out and ran away. Willie did a very good job of taking care of him. But we often can't control what an animal will do."

I closed my eyes and tried to pretend I was somewhere else. Anywhere.

"Is he dead?" somebody asked. A hush fell over the room.

"No, he's not dead," Mrs. Sweetly said. "He just ran away."

"Hey, Willie, how did it happen?" another kid asked.

"Yeah, where did he run to?"

I knew that I had to explain. I took a deep breath. I made myself think about Harriet Tubman. I stood up. Everybody was quiet when I spoke.

"It happened on Friday," I explained.

"Lester was scared, and I thought he wasn't feeling well. So when me and my sister Tina cleaned his cage, we put him on the grass. I thought it might make him feel better. Then he ran away."

There! I'd said it! Nobody moved. Nobody spoke.

"Why was Lester scared?" somebody asked.

I took another deep breath. This was the bad part. "I think it was because I let a lot of kids who live on my block pet him," I said.

"That was dumb," somebody said.

"I know," I said.

"Where did he go?" another kid asked.

"I don't know," I said. "I looked for him and looked for him, but he never came back."

I felt my eyes fill with tears. The last

thing I wanted to do was to cry, so I put my hands over my face so nobody would see me. Then I sat down and put my head on my desk.

I sat like that for about fifteen minutes. I heard kids talking quietly among themselves as they got in line to go to lunch.

"Willie," Mrs. Sweetly said in a very soft voice. "It's time for lunch." I picked up my head. Everybody was gone.

"I'm not hungry, I just want to stay here," I said.

Mrs. Sweetly sat down in the little seat beside me.

"Willie, I'd like you to have lunch with me. So we can talk about what happened," she said.

"I don't want to talk," I said.

"I think we should."

I didn't say anything, because I knew I didn't have a choice.

We got up and headed out the door. "Do you mind stopping by the teachers' room first? I have to get my lunch box," she said.

I was surprised to hear that Mrs. Sweetly had a lunch box. I thought teachers would call it something else.

"Mrs. Morris made some chocolate-chip cookies that she brought in this morning. Maybe you'd like one while you wait in the teachers' room," she said.

I looked straight ahead as I followed her down the hall. She opened the door to the teachers' room and we went in. I stood at the door for a moment. I was scared to go in, even with a teacher. Kids never get to go into the teachers' room.

Nearly all of the teachers I knew were

sitting around the table. Mrs. Morris was there, too. Mr. Gertz, the gym teacher, was doing a crossword puzzle. He looked up at me and grunted, which is what he always does. Ms. Avery, the music teacher, was listening to a CD player.

"Hi, everybody. Willie and I are having lunch today," Mrs. Sweetly said to the other teachers.

"Would you like a cookie, Willie?" Mrs. Morris asked. I was nervous because I was the only kid in the room, but I went over to get one anyway.

"Want some juice?" Mr. Gertz said over his newspaper.

"No, thank you," I said. He grunted and went back to his crossword.

I was so glad when Mrs. Sweetly got back so that we could leave.

Except for the sixth graders, who always ate last, the cafeteria was nearly empty. We took our lunch to a table far away from everybody else.

Mrs. Cotton had made our lunch this morning because my mom went to work early. I had a granola bar and egg-salad sandwiches, which are the worst sandwiches in the world. They can really smell up a lunch box. Mrs. Sweetly took out a carton of yogurt and an apple. Then she unwrapped a tuna-fish sandwich, which, except for peanut butter and honey, is one of my favorites. She must have seen my eyes light up when I saw her lunch.

"I'll trade if you throw in that granola bar," she said.

I couldn't believe it. Who would have

thought Mrs. Sweetly would know about trading?

When we had finished eating, Mrs. Sweetly said, "I was very touched about the things you wrote in your journal about Lester. It reminded me of something that happened to me when I was about your age."

I really didn't want to think about what had happened to Lester anymore, but I knew I had to listen.

"When I was in third grade, I had a dog named Blaze," Mrs. Sweetly continued. "He was an Irish setter. He was the most beautiful dog in the world. Anyway, he loved to run more than anything. And it was up to me to tie him up every night so he wouldn't run away. But he loved to run so much that one night I decided that I would let him run free, just for that night. So I didn't tie him up. But the next morning he had run so far away, I couldn't find him. I never saw him again."

I gasped when she said that. Mrs. Sweetly looked very sad. That made me sad too. I knew how bad she must have felt about Blaze because I had felt really bad about Lester, and I hadn't even liked him all that much.

She looked at me with a sad smile, and then said, "That happened so long ago, that I had almost forgotten it. But when I read what you wrote in your journal, it all came back. I felt I had let Blaze down, too."

"When did you stop feeling that way?" I asked.

"Well, I was sad for a long time. Then I was mad. I was mad at Blaze for running away and mad at myself for not tying him up as I was supposed to. But the more I thought about it, I realized that Blaze had run away because he was just being a dog, and that's what dogs do.

"You know, Willie, guinea pigs will be guinea pigs the same way dogs will be dogs."

"But I shouldn't have let all those kids pet Lester," I said.

She shook her head and smiled. "Part of growing up is making mistakes. It's also understanding how important it is to forgive someone who makes a mistake. Even when that person is you."

She took another bite of her apple. I took a bite out of one of Mrs. Morris's cookies. We sat there without saying much until it was time to go back to her room.

Nobody mentioned Lester when we came

back. I guess everybody knew I felt bad about him. But everybody was really curious about what the teachers' room was like, and everybody had a question. By the end of the day I was feeling better. About everything.

That night, in my very best writing, I wrote a note to Mrs. Sweetly in my journal:

> Dear Mrs. Sweetly,
>   Thank you for telling me about Blaze. I didn't like Lester as much as you liked Blaze, but just hearing about how you felt made me feel better, like I wasn't the only kid who had let a pet down. Thanks for sharing something that made you sad to make me unsad.

I didn't know if "unsad" was a word, but I didn't feel like looking it up. I figured she'd know what I meant. Then I borrowed a purple pencil from Tina's box and added:

You are one of the nicest teachers
I've had so far in my life.

After I finished writing, I went outside to look for Lester one last time. I wasn't really surprised when I didn't find him.

Before I left the backyard I yelled out as loud as I could, "I hope you're having fun wherever you are, Lester!"

Then I went back inside and ate my cone of mint-chocolate-chip ice cream with double-chocolate sprinkles.

Even after two and a half days in the freezer, it still tasted good.